Copyright © 1999 by Nord-Süd Verlag AG, Gossau Zürich, Switzerland
First published in Switzerland under the title Affenzoff

First published in the United States, Great Britain, Canada,
Australia, and New Zealand in 1999 by North-South Books,
an imprint of Nord-Süd Verlag AG, Gossau Zürich, Switzerland.

Distributed in the United States by North-South Books Inc., New York.

Library of Congress Cataloging-in-Publication Data is available.
A CIP catalogue record for this book is available from The British Library.

ISBN O-7358-1033-8 (trade binding)
ISBN O-7358-1034-6 (library binding)

Printed in Italy

For more information about our books, and the authors and artists
who create them, visit our web site: http://www.northsouth.com

A MICHAEL NEUGEBAUER BOOK
NORTH-SOUTH BOOKS · NEW YORK · LONDON

John A. Rowe

Monkey Trouble

THIS WAY

THAT WAY

Little Monkey was BIG trouble!
Little Monkey never listened.
He made faces and never did what he was told.

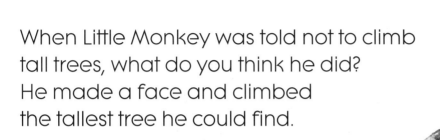

When Little Monkey was told not to climb
tall trees, what do you think he did?
He made a face and climbed
the tallest tree he could find.

The tall tree swayed like a ship's
mast in a terrible storm.
But Little Monkey wasn't afraid.

Little Monkey was *BIG* trouble. He threw nuts
and made faces, so Little Monkey didn't see the danger.

Little Monkey never listened.
So he didn't hear the wind huffing and puffing.

Little Monkey never listened.
So he didn't hear the wind rattling at windows and whistling
through keyholes.

Little Monkey never listened.
So he didn't hear the wind heading his way.

And while Little Monkey made faces and threw nuts,
the wind snuck up behind him.

"BOO!" said the wind. "SWOOSH!"

The gusty wind blew Little Monkey right out of the tree and sailed him across the sky like a lost hat.

Little Monkey's tiny body tumbled and turned through the air until he was far, far away.

Oh, if only he had listened … !

Suddenly… Little Monkey began to drop.
Fast…
Faster…
And faster…
"Help…" The wind stole his words away.

"Boo hoo…" The wind dried up his tears.

Little Monkey was BIG trouble all right. But he was lucky, too . . .

Platsssh!
Little Monkey landed on something soft and warm.

"Hello," it said sleepily, "I'm a new baby girl."
Then she began to snore loudly.

The stork guided them safely to the ground on a fluffy cloud.
Little Monkey popped his head out for a look.

"Ooooooh!" cried excited voices, "it's our new baby girl."
And Little Monkey was swept up and smothered in BIG wet kisses.

"No...no...not ME!"

Little Monkey tried to explain, but the proud parents were far too
excited to listen. They cuddled him and sniffed him and dressed
him in a beautiful pink dress.

Oh, if only he had listened...!

Soon Little Monkey was running down the road
as fast as he could.
But how would he find his way back home again?

After a while he sat down for a rest.

"Look out! Look out!" roared a shaggy lion.
"Little girls shouldn't sit there.
Someone might pounce on them."

"I'm NOT a little girl," answered Little Monkey,
"and I'm looking for the way home."

So the shaggy lion let Little Monkey ride on his back.
But every time that shaggy lion let out a great big roar,
Little Monkey's ears hurt.

Oh, if only he had listened . . . !

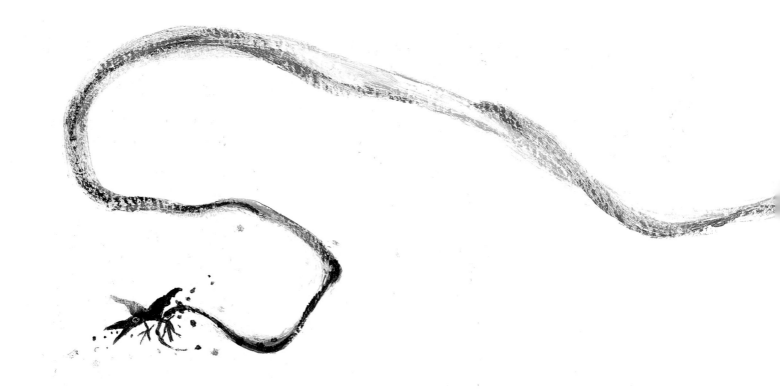

Soon Little Monkey was running down the road
as fast as he could.
After a while he sat down for a rest.

"Look out! Look out!" hooted a hopalong kangaroo.
"Little girls shouldn't sit there. Someone might jump on them."

"I'm NOT a little girl," answered Little Monkey, "and I'm looking
for the way home."

So the kangaroo let Little Monkey ride in her pouch.
But every time that kangaroo took a great big hop,
Little Monkey bounced around like a basketball.

Oh, if only he had listened . . . !

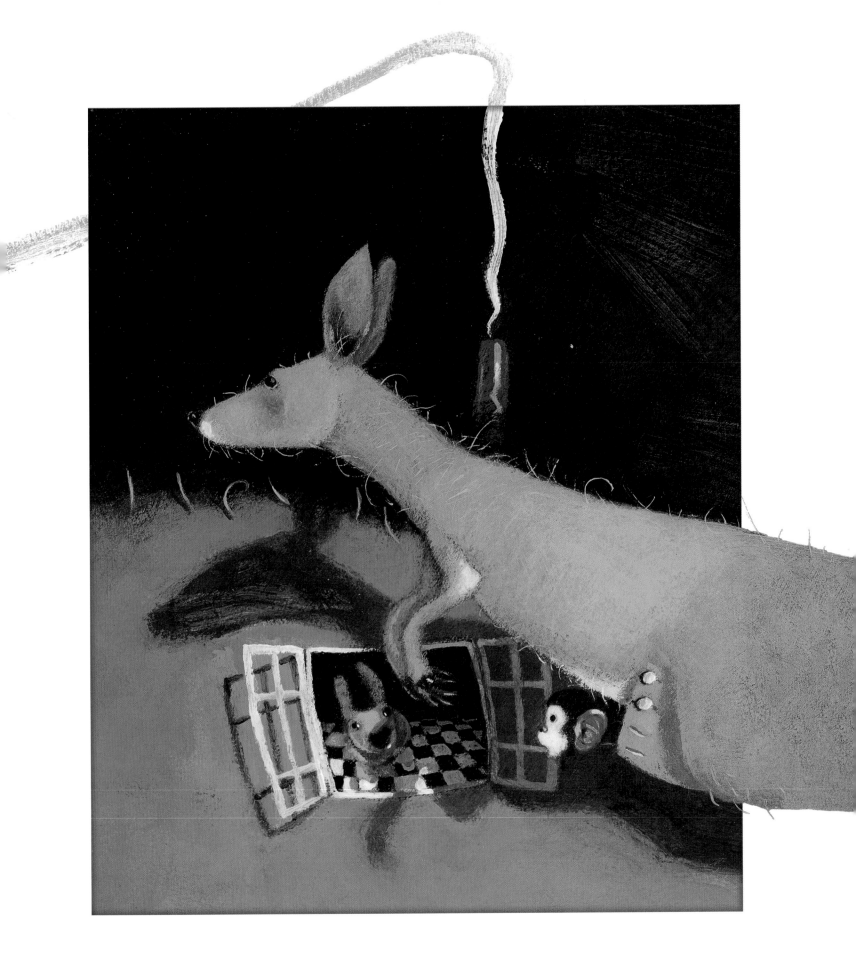

Soon Little Monkey was running down the road as fast
as he could.
After a while he sat down for a rest.

"Look out! Look out!" snorted a tattered old horse.
"Little girls shouldn't sit there. Someone might gallop on them."

"I'm NOT a little girl," answered Little Monkey, "and I'm looking
for the way home."

So the horse let Little Monkey ride on his back.
But every time that horse felt tired, he sat down
and Little Monkey fell off.

Oh, if only he had listened...!

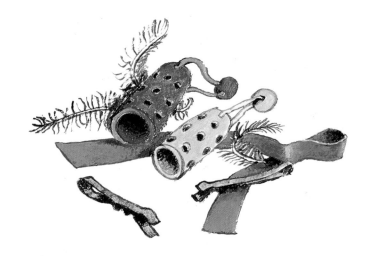

Soon Little Monkey was running down the road as fast
as he could.
After a while he sat down for a rest.

"Look out! Look out!" screeched a feathery ostrich.
"Little girls shouldn't sit there. Someone might step on them."

"I'm NOT a little girl," answered Little Monkey, "and I'm looking
for the way home."

So the feathery ostrich let Little Monkey ride on her back.
But every time that feathery ostrich stooped and buried her
head, Little Monkey got sand up his nose.

Oh, if only he had listened . . . !

Soon Little Monkey was running down the road as fast as he could.
After a while he sat down for a rest.

"Look out! Look out!" squawked a wide-winged pelican.
"Little girls shouldn't sit there. Someone might land on them."

"I'm NOT a little girl," answered Little Monkey, "and I'm looking
for the way home."

So the wide-winged pelican let Little Monkey ride in his bill.
And every time that pelican flapped his wide wings,
Little Monkey held on tighter.

Little Monkey was just beginning to think that he would never
ever find his way home when all of a sudden a tall tree
appeared in the distance.

"That's it!" cried Little Monkey excitedly. "That's my home."

And what excitement there was when Little Monkey's mother and father and brothers and sisters and all of his friends saw him again.

"It's me! It's me!" cried Little Monkey. "I'm not really a little girl." And he made a face to show them that it truly was him.

That night they threw a big party to celebrate Little Monkey's safe return. All the animals were there and they gave him a special present.

A wonderful coat decorated with large stones. Now Little Monkey was so heavy, no gusty wind could ever blow him away again.

Little Monkey was BIG trouble!
When told not to swim in the deep pond, what do you think he did?

Oh . . . will he EVER listen?

Little Monkey was BIG trouble all right.
But he was lucky, too . . .

Do not
lift
this flap!